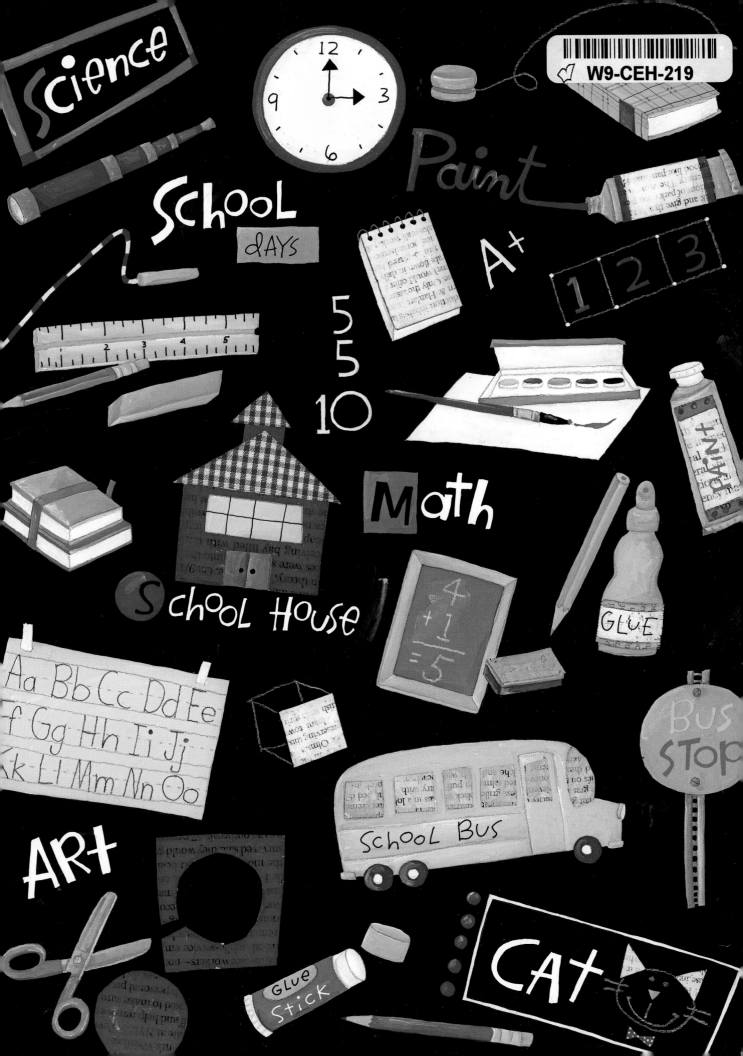

To Alison Anthoine, for all her help,
support, and advice over the years

Henry Holt and Company, LLC, *Publishers since 1866*
175 Fifth Avenue, New York, New York 10010
www.henryholtchildrensbooks.com

Henry Holt® is a registered trademark of Henry Holt and Company, LLC.
Copyright © 2007 by Nancy Wolff
All rights reserved.
Distributed in Canada by H. B. Fenn and Company Ltd.

Library of Congress Cataloging-in-Publication Data
Wolff, Nancy.
It's time for school with Tallulah / by Nancy Wolff.—1st ed.
p.   cm.
Summary: Includes directions for making Tallulah's Snackitty Crackers.
Summary: Tallulah the cat plays school with her friends, from welcoming a new
student, through naptime, snacks, and chores, to posing for a class picture.
ISBN-13: 978-0-8050-7962-3 / ISBN-10: 0-8050-7962-9
[1. Schools—Fiction. 2. Cats—Fiction. 3. Dogs—Fiction.] I. Title. II. Title:
It is time for school with Tallulah.
PZ7.W821255It 2007   [E]—dc22   2006030769

First Edition—2007
Printed in the United States of America on acid-free paper. ∞
The artist used gouache on Canson paper
to create the illustrations for this book.

10 9 8 7 6 5 4 3 2 1

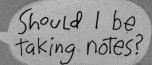

It's Time for School

with TALLULAH

NANCY
WOLFF

Henry Holt and Company
New York

Tallulah was born to teach.

She likes to share her most interesting tidbits of knowledge with her good friends Roxy and Freddie and her dog, Flapjack. Today, a new student will be joining the class. Everyone is very excited.

FIRE EXTINGUISHER

Before school begins, Tallulah sets up her classroom. She cleans the chalkboard and arranges desks and chairs. Now everything is in order for a day of learning.

Teacher

Freddie

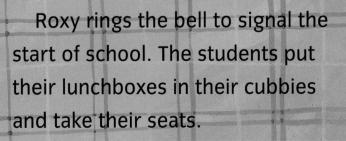

Roxy rings the bell to signal the start of school. The students put their lunchboxes in their cubbies and take their seats.

Tallulah introduces Nigel and invites him to take off his scarf. Then she goes over the rules of the class.

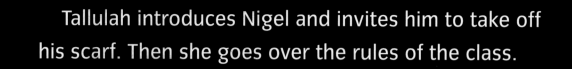

CLASS RULES

1. Class participation is always welcome, as long as you raise your hand, hoof, paw, or wing (no tails, please).

2. Share supplies, not germs.

3. No yelling, pushing, biting, or tail pulling.

4. Proper attire is appreciated (especially on class picture afternoon).

Teacher

Attendance is the first order of the day. After roll call,
Tallulah and her class move on to the welcome song.

(Works best if sung to the tune of "Happy Birthday.")

Good morning to you,
bonjour and hola, too.
Meow everybody,
and how do you do?

Tallulah asks the students to tell a little something
about themselves to make Nigel feel comfortable.

She begins by sharing her passion for inventing new recipes and describes her latest sandwich experiment—banana, cucumber, and sardines on toast.

Freddie loves pickles, and his favorite color is green.

Roxy admits her tail is not naturally curly, and she enjoys a nice mud bath at least once a week.

So far, I've only been around the block, but a dog can dream—can't he?

Flapjack is crazy about exotic foods—Hungarian goulash, to be specific—and wants to travel and see more of the world.

Once, I caught a catfish, but I threw it back.

Nigel seems shy but manages to squeak out that he enjoys fishing.

It's journal time, so Tallulah asks Flapjack to pass out paper. Today, they practice writing their names and find it's not as easy as it looks.

...OR does the L come before the E?

Freddie volunteers to collect the papers and helps hang them up on the bulletin board before story time.

I hope neatness doesn't count.

Tallulah gathers everyone in a circle
and reads aloud from her favorite book.

After a lively story discussion, Tallulah invites
the class to check out a book from the library.

It's snack time, at last. Hooray! Thinking can really build up an appetite. Roxy passes out juice, while Tallulah helps the class assemble a special treat.

Playtime follows snack, so everyone helps with cleanup.

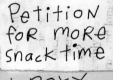

Petition
for more
Snack time
1. ROXY
2. Freddie
3. ⠶⠶
4. NiGEL

CREAM CHEESE

Raisins

Tallulah gets ready for arts and crafts,
while the rest of the class makes a beeline
for the play area.

VOTE ROXY for class President

SUPPLY CLOSET

GLUE and TAPE

SEQUINS SPARKLES

ART SMOCKS

PAINTS

Nigel and Freddie construct a submarine for tracking undersea treasures. Roxy raids the dress-up box and then creates a throne fit for a plaid princess. Flapjack builds a spaceship that will bring him one step closer to being the first dog on the moon.

I don't kiss frogs—EVER!

Blast off

The craft project of the day is to design placemats. Tallulah prepares the paint jars and dips into her special supply of sparkles and sequins. After the classroom is tidied up from playtime, Roxy, Freddie, Nigel, and Flapjack join Tallulah at the craft table to begin work on their mats.

GLUE
STICK

When the mats are finished, Tallulah hangs them up to dry.

The art supplies are returned to their proper place and Nigel is picked to be first for show-and-tell. Once over his stage fright, Nigel discovers he likes an audience.

Roxy goes next and holds up the blue ribbon she won in a talent show for her crowd-pleasing performance on the ukulele of "Twist and Shout."

It's lunchtime, so Freddie and Flapjack save their show-and-tell for another day. Tallulah rings the lunch bell and everyone takes a turn washing at the sink. After a cleanliness inspection, they each collect their lunches and placemats and return to their desks.

Roxy and Flapjack enjoy cream cheese and grape jelly sandwiches, while Freddie munches on lettuce, pickles, and mint jelly. Nigel is delighted to discover Tallulah shares his fondness for tuna. Before long, Tallulah asks Roxy to ring the bell for recess.

Do You want to share some of my green Jell-O?

The class lines up and Tallulah leads the way outside with her
kitty version of the bunny hop, which is more leaping than hopping.

Today they play a favorite game of Tallulah's called cat and mouse.

Meow Meow

GAME RULES

The cat, in this case Tallulah, runs after the mice—Freddie, Roxy, Nigel, and Flapjack—and tries to tag them. When a mouse is tagged, she becomes a cat and joins the other cat(s) in chasing down the rest of the mice. The cats must meow so the mice know who they are. The last mouse left is the winner and starts out as the cat in the next round.

Tallulah sees her students are getting tired. As luck would have it, naptime is next on the schedule. Freddie lets Nigel have the green mat.

The green mat always works for me.

I'm too wound up to sleep.

After nap is over, the class works on adding numbers. Two of Roxy's buttons plus four on Freddie's shirt make six buttons altogether.

HINT: A wise teacher uses all available tools to make learning as interesting as possible.

Now it's on to the class chores. Freddie updates the weather chart,

while Roxy gives Nigel pointers on the care and feeding of Goldie,

and Tallulah and Flapjack water the bean seeds.

Learning new things about the world and each other is wonderful. Spending the day with old friends and making a new one is even better. But what fun would attending school be without a class picture to add to the photo album!

At the end of the day, Tallulah is pleased to see that Nigel has finally taken off his scarf. Tallulah rings the bell and dismisses the class. Nigel asks to take over ringing the bell.

May I please ring the bell?

Maybe someday Tallulah will have a big school with
a well-equipped playground and a bus for field trips.
For now, she's happy sharing what she knows with
Freddie, Roxy, Nigel, Flapjack, and anyone else who
wants to join the fun.

Hey, Nigel—
do you want
to walk home
with us?